I0606816

Charles Hallock

A Complete Biographical Sketch of Stonewall Jackson

Charles Hallock

A Complete Biographical Sketch of Stonewall Jackson

ISBN/EAN: 9783337226251

Printed in Europe, USA, Canada, Australia, Japan

Cover: Foto ©Raphael Reischuk / pixelio.de

A COMPLETE
BIOGRAPHICAL SKETCH
OF
"Stonewall" Jackson:

GIVING A

FULL AND ACCURATE ACCOUNT

OF THE

Leading Events of his Military Career,

HIS DYING MOMENTS,

AND

THE OBSEQUIES

AT

RICHMOND AND LEXINGTON.

AUGUSTA, GA.:
STEAM POWER-PRESS CHRONICLE AND SENTINEL.
1863.

PREFACE.

While the great heart of the country mourns with inconsolable grief the affliction it has so recently suffered in the death of its idolized chieftain, it is natural that the desire should be earnest and universal to learn more of his history and personal worth. To meet this popular desire, this unpretending little volume is now brought before the public; and in so cheap a form as to place it within the reach of all. It purports to be nothing more than an outline sketch of the life and character of the hero, soldier, and Christian, together with full details of his dying hours and the honors paid to his memory by his bereaved and devoted countrymen. For the facts so hastily drawn together, the author has had to depend, in a considerable degree, upon the published newspaper accounts, although much that appears in these pages, it is believed, is new to the public. The work is necessarily meagre, from its very conciseness, yet embraces the leading events in the life of the illustrious subject of the sketch.

CHARLES HALLOCK

Augusta, May 28th, 1863.

JACKSON.

"What needs our hero for his honoured bones,
The labour of an age in piled stones?
Or that his hallowed reliques should be hid
Under a starry-pointing pyramid?
Dear son of memory, great heir of fame,
What need'st thou such weak witness of thy name?"

Now is the name of JACKSON doubly enshrined in the hearts of the nation. Of all the names renowned in the history of the *Old* Republic, few shine out with brighter lustre than Jackson. The "hero of New Orleans" fills a prominent place in the memory of a grateful people. But Jackson, and Washington, and Jefferson, and Calhoun, with all that galaxy of illustrious names, *Southern* names, to which we have been taught from childhood to look with pride and admiration, must now be regarded by the people of this Confederacy as belonging to an era that is past. Of this noble heritage we must yield to others a share in common with ourselves. But the Jackson that we are now called upon to mourn is *peculiarly our own.* He is identified with the history of the young Republic. He was one of the instruments appointed to give her form and substance and being, and a place among the nations of the earth. With his strong right hand he helped her to throw off the tyrants' chain, and carved out for her a path to honor. His precious blood is the price of our liberty.

Henceforth no titles shall be employed to designate the man. The name is of itself distinctive—a tower of strength, a monolith of fame. The succeeding generation will know no other Jackson, and infant lips will lisp the word with the same mysterious feeling of reverence that prompted us when we spelled out the name of "The Father of his Country." Yet we will not blot out the memory of the past, nor permit one luminary of the present day to eclipse the glories of the old regime; but choosing the immortal WASHINGTON as the bright particular star of our earlier hopes and civilization, and STONEWALL JACKSON of the present, dip our pen in the sunlight, and write them side by side in the unclouded sky of heaven's blue vault.

General THOMAS JONATHAN JACKSON was born in Clarksburg, Harrison county, Virginia, on the 21st day of January, 1824. His great-grandfather, John Jackson, and his great-grandmother, were of English birth.

They emigrated to this country at an early day, and settled on the south branch of the Potomac. Subsequently they removed to what is now Lewis county, in Northwestern Virginia. Their son, Edward, (grandfather of Thomas J.,) was surveyor in Harrison county for many years, and subsequently represented the county of Lewis in the Legislature for several years. Jonathan Jackson, the father of Gen. Jackson, studied law under Judge John C. Jackson, in Clarksburg; and then commenced its practice, acquiring some reputation. He became embarrassed as security for his friends, and all his property was swept away before his death, which took place in 1827. He left four children, of whom Thomas, the youngest, was but three years old. An uncle, then residing in Lewis county, took the little orphan to live with him. Here Thomas, by going to school three months in the winter, and laboring on the farm the residue of the year, as was the custom with farmers' sons in Western Virginia, acquired the rudiments of a plain English education. About the age of seventeen he was appointed to a Cadetship at West Point. He here graduated with high distinction, in 1846, being then in the 23d year of his age.

War having broken out between the United States and Mexico, Jackson at once entered the military service under Gen. Zachary Taylor, with the rank of Brevet Lieutenant. When Gen. Scott was ordered to Mexico, Lieut. Jackson joined him at Vera Cruz. At the siege of that city, he commanded a battery, and attracted attention by the coolness and judgment with which he worked his guns, and was promoted to the rank of first Lieutenant. Afterwards, at the battle of Cerro Gordo, he was brevetted Captain. Some time after that hotly-contested engagement and brilliant victory of the American arms, his old comrade, General, then Captain J Bankhead Magruder, was placed in command of a battery of six light pieces. Capt. Magruder, 1st Artillery, had led the storming party under Gen. Harney up the heights of Cerro Gordo. He was the first artillery officer who entered the enemy's works, sword in hand—had captured the guns and turned them on the retreating foe. Gen. Scott rode into the works and addressing Capt. M., said: "Captain, you have won these guns; they are yours; your ardent wish for a light battery can be gratified. Take these guns and mount them. They shall henceforth be Magruder's battery"

Jackson bore an active and conspicuous part in all the battles of the war that followed, and especially in the decisive engagement that resulted in the capture of the city of Mexico and the triumphant entry of the American army within its gates. When that army was advancing towards the city, on its march from Contreras, Lieutenant Jackson reported to Captain Magruder for duty in his battery, having obtained at last the desired transfer to the light artillery. Magruder placed him immediately in command of a section of the battery, and, conspicuous for his skill and courage, assigned him to a separate position in the assault on the city. With characteristic valor and impetuosity, he boldly assailed the defenses at the San Cosme gate of the city, and contributed powerfully, by his skill and well directed fire, to the subsequent capture of the Capital. His signal services were duly chronicled in the official report of Capt. Magruder and the formal and full report of Gen. Scott, as the records of the United States Government will show. The motive of his ardent desire to join Magruder's battery was stated by him to a friend at the close of the war, and is characteristic. He said : "I wanted to see active service. I wished to be near the enemy, and in the fight ; and when I heard John Magruder had got his battery, I bent all my energies to be with him, for I knew if there was any fighting to be done, Magruder would be on hand."

He had previously been rewarded with successive promotions for his gallantry and merit, and, for his bravery and skill on this occasion, took rank as Brevet Major. The Army Register and the actual history and facts of the Mexican war do not furnish the name of another person entering the war without position or office who attained the high rank of major in the brief campaign and series of battles from Vera Cruz to the city of Mexico.

At the close of the Mexican war, Jackson served for a brief period in Florida, and then resigned his position in the army because of impaired health, and in 1851 received the unanimous appointment from the Board of Vistors, of Professor of Natural and Experimental Philosophy and Instructor of Artillery in the Virginia Military Institute, at Lexington. Some very curious circumstances were connected with his appointment to this chair. When the vacancy occurred which Jackson was destined to fill, Gen. Smith, the superintendent, was instructed by the Board of Visitors to seek, by private inquiries, some one suitable for the position. Among those to whom he first applied was Gen. D. H. Hill, then a professor in Washington College, we believe. Hill warmly recommended T. J. Jackson, then serving in the army in Florida. Hill at that time had no family connection with Jackson ; but he knew him well, and with a penetration and sagacity that did him much credit, declared that he was not only a competent, faithful, reliable man, but had a great deal of "outcome" in him.

Repairing subsequently to West Point, Gen. Smith addressed his inquiries to the faculty there. They recommended as eligible for the position, McClellan, Rosecranz, Foster, Peck, and Gustavus W. Smith ; the first four now noted Federal Generals, and the last an officer of high rank in our own service, until his late resignation. Upon Gen Smith's stating that Jackson had been recommended, they said of him that he was an indefatigable man, and would do well ; but he had come to the academy badly prepared. Inquiries at New York and Fortress Monroe further developed the fact, that the persons recommended at West Point were considered better *book-men* than Jackson, but all bore testimony to Jackson's great personal worth and energy, and his sterling qualities.

When the Board of Visitors met, General Smith reported the name of Jackson to the Board, together with a statement of the recommendations and encomiums already referred to.

It happened that there was on the Board a member who appeared there on that occasion for the first time and the last. He at once advocated Jackson's appointment, though evidently taken by surprise at the suggestion of his name. He spoke in very high terms of Jackson, whose townsman he said he was, and told of the great pleasure which his appointment would give to the people of Northwest Virginia. The man who thus eulogized Jackson was J. S. Carlile. He was the only one of the Board who knew Jackson, and he warmly advocated him before that jury of strangers.

Influenced by what they had thus heard, the Board, without the usual delays, at once ordered the appointment to be tendered to Jackson. The state of his health at the time aided in causing him to accept it

Of the gifted men with whom Jackson was thus brought into comparison, and to whom he was adjudged by all, save Hill and his Virginia friends, to be inferior, which one has he not immeasurably outstripped? They were ranked before him, but the inspiration within him, which needed only occasion to develop it, swiftly asserted its authority. Jackson will live in the admiration of the world and the affections of a great Republic, long after those whose prospects for fame and distinction seemed fairer, shall have been even forgotten! *They* have taken high rank in the Federal army, but already have the infamous deeds of some of them made their names a hissing and a reproach among men and nations.

Jackson's services at Lexington were not conspicuous. Colonel Gilham was considered as the military genius of the school, and Thomas Jackson was but little thought of by the small hero-worshipers of Lexington. He, however, labored assiduously and with scrupulous fidelity in the duties of the important offices he filled during the ten years of his Professorship, and gave to his native State the valued and substantial service of his modest and unobtrusive, but public spirited and useful life. Here he became a Soldier of the Cross; and, as a humble, conscientious and useful christian man, he established the character which has developed into the world-renowned christian hero. The cadets of the Institute had but little partiality for the taciturn, praying professor. He was stern in the performance of his duty. At one time his life was threatened by a cadet who had been dismissed from the Institute for misdemeanor, the wild boy actually going to the extremity of laying in wait for him on the road leading from the Institute to the village. As Jackson in his accustomed walk towards the village, approached the spot where his enemy awaited him, a bystander called out to him of his danger. And here was manifested that peculiar trait—an utter fearlessness or indifference to danger, which has since so often shone out upon many a battle-field. Perhaps it was a real indifference to life, or more probably, an implicit trust which he placed in the Divine Being to shield him from harm. "Let the assassin murder, if he will," replied the Professor quietly, as he walked in the most unconcerned manner towards the young man, who slunk abashed from his path.

Perhaps none of the acquaintances of Jackson were more surprised at his brilliant exhibitions of genius in this war, than those who knew his blank life at the Institute, and were familiar with the stiff and uninteresting figure that was to be seen every Sunday in a pew of the Presbyterian Church at Lexington. But true genius awaits occasion commensurate with its power and aspiration. The spirit of Jackson was trained in another school than that of West Point or Lexington, and had it been confined there, it never would have illuminated the page of history. But to the corps of Cadets of the Virginia Military Institute, what a legacy he has left; what an example of all that is good and great and true in the character of a Christian Soldier!

We come now to the most eventful period of his eventful life—a period of painful interest to every citizen of this Confederacy, and one in which each, however obscure, has borne his humble part.

When the first harsh note of war called our country's sons to battle, Jackson repaired at once to Richmond, where he was commissioned Colonel by Gov Letcher, and attached to Gen. Johnston's command on the Upper Potomac. Directly after, being ordered to take command at Harper's Ferry, he reached that post on May 2d, 1861, and the next day entered upon his duties. From that time until the memorable day on which he received his fatal wound, he was never absent from service. That was the 3d of May, 1863, completing the exact period of two years of unremitting toil.

At Falling Waters, on the 2d of July, 1861, he engaged the advance of Patterson, and gave the Yankees one of the first exemplifications of his ready-witted strategy; as Patterson never knew, that for several hours, he was fighting an insignificant force, skillfully disposed to conceal their weakness, while Johnston was making his dispositions in the rear.

The first conspicuous services of Jackson in this war were rendered at Manassas, in 1861; although the marks of active determination he had shown on the Upper Potomac, and the affair of Falling Waters, had already secured for him promotion to a Brigadier Generalship. Just previous to that battle, perhaps better known as the Battle of Bull Run, when the troops under his command had made a forced march, on halting at night, they fell on the ground exhausted and faint. The hour arrived for setting the watch for the night. The officer of the day went to the General's tent, and said, "General, the men are all wearied, and there is not one but is asleep. Shall I wake them?"

"No!" said the noble Jackson, "let them sleep, and I will watch the camp to-night."

And all night long he rode round that lonely camp, the one lone sentinel for that brave, but weary and silent host of Virginia heroes. And when glorious morning broke, the soldiers woke refreshed, and ready for action, all unconscious of the noble vigils kept over their slumber.

A similar instance is related, when Jackson occupied a small farm house on a certain night, and allowed his under officers to sleep, while he spent the passing hours in prayer, walking the turnpike before the quarters, or looking in at intervals upon the men,—until just before dawn, when a vacated place upon an unhung gate afforded him a short season of rest.

Again, in a house that was used as a temporary hospital, he exercised a kindly care and supervision of the wounded men, moving quietly among the sufferers, and administering to their wants with tender solicitude.

Manifold and touching are the anecdotes like these, illustrative of the noble character of Jackson, of his self-denial, and kindly regard for the comfort and welfare of his men. No wonder that they loved him, or that his example excited in their breasts a spirit of emulation to do or dare aught that the exigencies of the occasion might demand! No wonder that they valued his approving nod more than the fulsome praise that others might bestow!

That he was not unmindful either of the sufferings of his foes, the testimony of the Federal nurse bears witness,—who has contrasted in glowing colors his prompt assistance and sympathy with the tardiness and indifference of McDowell, who had left his wounded to the tender mercies of their enemies. The case of the men was urgent and wrought upon the sympathies of Jackson, who could not see them suffer and die from neglect; and he himself provided for their comfort and relief. The story is told in Northern papers. Equally sensitive was his regard for the rights of property. He allowed no trespass which military necessity did not absolutely require. On one occasion he caused a young soldier who had captured a Yankee, to return to the prisoner an overcoat which he had appropriated to supply a positive need during a heavy rain storm. Instances might be multiplied, but these will suffice to illustrate the character of our hero.

Jackson spoke his first immortal words at Manassas, when he stayed the retreat of our forces just as it verged on irretrievable disaster. The enemy were pressing hard. Overwhelmed by superior numbers (the record runs,) and compelled to yield before a fire that swept everything before it, the heroic Gen. Bee rode up and down his lines, encouraging his troops by everything that was dear to them, to stand up and repel the tide which threatened them with destruction. At last his own brigade dwindled away to a mere handfull, with every field officer killed or disabled. He rode up to Gen. Jackson, and said: "General, they are beating us back!"

"No, sir!" replied the invincible, as his eyes blazed with a victorious courage, "We'll give them the bayonet!"

Gen. Bee immediately rallied the remnant of his brigade, and his last words to them were: "*There is Jackson standing like a stone-wall.* Let us determine to die here, and we will conquer. Follow me!"

Scarcely had he spoken these memorable words, when he fell dead upon the field; but their utterance proved a legacy to the immortal Jackson and his lion-hearted Brigade more highly prized than any gifts within the power of kings or potentates to bestow, because associated with heroic achievements and deeds of valor, and victories wrung from the category of impossibilities. The homely soubriquet of "Stonewall" will live in history long after generations yet to come shall have passed away—will gleam with living fire when bronze shall have corroded and marble crumbled into dust.* The rout and panic that thereafter followed have already become a part of the annals of the new Republic.

Jackson's fame was now fully established. But in the meeds so nobly won was embraced a moral triumph not less signal than the victory he had gained over the foes of his country. The eminent qualifications of a great commander, which he had shown himself to possess, dashed to atoms the insinuations that had been made as to his lack of capacity, and brought a blush of shame to the cheeks of those who made merry at the first apparition of the future hero on the battle field. His queer figure on horseback, and the habit of settling his chin in his stock, were very amusing to some who made a flippant jest of the military specimen of the Old Dominion. The jest is forgiven and forgotten in the tributes of admiration and love which were to ensue to the popular hero o the war.

If the truth be told, however, Jackson was not an elegant rider. He sat stifly in the saddle, with arms akimbo and legs rigidly straightened before him, and toes pointing zenith-ward; and when his beast started off on his inevitable lope, the General's body swayed in accompaniment, with an awkward jerking motion, as though a stiff spring had been inserted beneath the back of his saddle. Neither was his bearing altogether martial, and not improved by the shocking slouched hat that he almost invariably wore.

The truth is, that Jackson was not educated in Mr. Turvydrop's school of politeness, nor versed in the poetry of motion. His was that true politeness which is prompted by a kindly heart, and consists not in graceful postures or sickening grimaces, but in benevolent acts and endeavors to increase the happiness of one's fellows. Indeed, his soldiers came to love him for his very eccentricities, albeit they at times provoked a smile. He was always cheered when under the eye of the army, and on such occasions loped away as fast as he could with his body bent forward, and

*See Appendix A.

holding his hat out stiffly before him, by way of a salute, like a rusty-jointed collector of contributions at a protracted meeting. He seemed embarrassed by any marked courtesies extended to him.

But Jackson was not always indifferent to his personal attire. There were occasions on which he bestowed more than usual attention to his dress, and then his appearance was commanding, and even elegant. It is affirmed by many who were familiar with his habits, that this special regard to his attire was an infallible sign of an approaching battle. Even so on the day before he received his fatal wound; his coat and pants were of the usual greyish blue, but of the finest quality, and the gold-lace fancy work on his sleeve looked as if it might have been put on the day before; his boots were well glossed and his spurs looked like burnished gold. He wore buck gloves with cuffs that came half-way up to his elbows, and a black felt hat of the fashion usually worn by officers. His costume was most befitting to his rank, and he looked every inch the officer that he was.

One of the most remarkable expeditions and marches of Jackson was in the depth of the winter of 1861-'2, when he was sent from Gen. Johnston's lines to Winchester.

On the first of January, 1862, he marched with his command from Winchester to Bath, in Morgan county, and from the latter place to Romney where there had been a large Federal force for many weeks, and from which point they had committed extensive depredations on the surrounding country. Gen. Jackson drove the enemy from Romney and the neigboring country without much fighting. His troops, however, endured the severest hardships in the expedition. Their sufferings were terrible in what was the severest portion of the winter. They were compelled at one time to struggle through an almost blinding storm of snow and sleet, and to bivouac at night in the forests, without tents or camp equipage. Many of the troops were frozen on the march, and died from exposure and exhaustion.

In this terrible expedition Jackson gave the most remarkable proofs of his grim energy in the field and the iron mould in which he was cast. His men were becoming acquainted with the habits of their commander. He appeared to be a man of almost superhuman endurance. Neither heat nor cold made the slightest impression upon him. Good quarters and dainty fare were as nothing to him. He lived as his soldiers lived, and endured all the fatigue and all the suffering that they endured. He partook of but few social enjoyments. Never absent a single day from duty, he did everything with the quiet, stern energy of an iron will.

> "A frame of adamant, a soul of fire,
> No dangers fright him and no labors tire;
> O'er love, o'er fear, extends his wide domain,
> Unconquered lord of pleasure and of pain.
> No joys to him pacific sceptres yield:
> War sounds the trump, he rushes to the field."

Without doubt, the most brilliant and extraordinary passage in the military life of General Jackson was the ever famous campaign of the summer of 1862 in the Valley of Virginia. That campaign, in which, in the short space of one month, he drove back into the enemy's territory FOUR Generals, with large captures in prisoners and stores, made the most brilliant part of his reputation. In a few weeks the name of Jackson mounted to the zenith of fame. In dramatic effects, in rapid incidents and in swift and sudden renown, his name challenged comparison with the most extraordinary phenomena in the annals of military genius.

In the spring of 1862, Gen. Jackson had been placed in command of the small army of observation which held the upper valley of the Shenandoah and the country about Staunton. It was intended that he should remain *quasi* inactive, to watch the enemy and wait for him; but he soon commenced maneuvering on his own responsibility, and ventured upon a scale of operations that threw the higher military authorities at Richmond into a fever of anxiety and alarm.

In less than thirty days he dashed at Fremont's advance, west of Staunton, and driving it back, wheeled his army, swept down the Valley and drove Banks across the Potomac. Returning to the upper Valley, he maneuvered around for three weeks—in the meantime dealing Fremont a heavy blow at Cross Keys and defeating Shields in the Luray Valley—and then suddenly swept down the Virginia Central Railroad, via Gordonsville, on McClellan's right, before Richmond.

His own official report of this splendid exploit is characteristic, and testifies to his modesty and unselfishness, and the humility with which he accepted the victories he won as manifest tokens of the gracious favor with which Heaven regarded our cause. He took no credit to himself, but ascribed all success to the intrepid valor and endurance of his soldiers and to the will of Providence. It is dated—

"HEADQUARTERS, WINCHESTER, May 26, 1862.

"Within four weeks this army has made long and rapid marches, fought six combats and two battles, signally defeating the enemy in each one, captured several stands of colors and pieces of artillery, with numerous prisoners, and vast medical, ordnance, and army stores, and finally driven the boastful host, which was ravaging our beautiful country, into utter rout. The General Commanding would warmly express to the officers and men under his command, his joy in their achievement, and his thanks for their brilliant gallantry in action and their patient obedience under the hardships of forced marches, often more painful to the brave soldier than the dangers of battle.

"The explanation of the severe exertions to which the Commanding General called the army, which were endured by them with such cheerful confidence in him, is now given in the victory of yesterday. He receives this proof of their confidence in the past with pride and gratitude, and asks only a similar confidence in the future. But his chief duty to-day, and that of the army, is to recognize devoutly the hand of a protecting Providence in the brilliant successes of the last three days, which have given us the results of a great victory without great losses, and to make the oblation of our thanks to God for his mercies to us and our country, in heart-felt acts of religious worship. For this purpose, the troops will remain in camp to-day, suspending, as far as practicable, all military exercises, and the chaplains of regiments will hold divine service in their several charges at four o'clock, P. M., to-day.

"Per order," etc.

The soldiers of that Brigade will cherish this simple order of their General as a most sacred heir-loom, and teach their children's children to trace out with their infant fingers the precious words. How faithfully they gave him that simple confidence he asked, their subsequent career has abundantly shown. Illustrious commander! noble men!

The part that Jackson played in winding up the campaign on the Peninsula is well known; how anxiously, day after day, his advent was awaited by the Confederate forces that were battling with McClellan's overwhelming host; how they at last utterly despaired of his coming; how victory then seemed trembling in the balance, and the Confederates, sorely pressed and wavering, were on the point of yielding the field; how he unexpectedly arrived at this critical juncture, after a most rapid and toilsome march, and crossing the Chickahominy just at the nick of time, fell upon McClellan's flank and rear, and dealt him such blows as drove him from his position; how he dashed from point to point, always in the thickest of the fight and just where his services were needed most; and how, after a sanguinary conflict of several hours, he succeeded in capturing all the batteries on his front, consisting of eighteen guns, and ceased at last from his labors only when the enemy, discomfited and confused, was driven ingloriously to the cover of his gunboats.

Since that memorable and decisive series of battles before Richmond, the military services of Jackson have been many and valuable; but they are comparatively fresh in the recollections of the public. It is proper, however, to notice the distinct part which he took in the summer campaign against Pope; as we do not believe that justice has been done to Jackson's contribution to the Second Battle of Manassas.

At the outset of this campaign, it was probably the design of Gen. Lee, with the bulk of the Confederate army, to take the front, left and right, and engage Gen. Pope at or near the Rapidan, while Jackson and Ewell were to cross the Shenandoah river and mountains, cut off his supplies by way of the railroad, and menace his rear. It will at once be noticed that this adventure, on the part of Jackson, was difficult and desperate; it took the risk of any new movements of Pope, by which he (Jackson) himself might be cut off. It was obvious, indeed, that if Pope could reach Gordonsville, he would cut off Jackson's supplies, and this risk had to be taken by the intrepid commander.

Cedar Mountain was fought and won from Pope before he knew the campaign was opened. Jackson fell back, but only to flank him on the right. Pope retired from the Rapidan to the Rappahannock, but Jackson swung still further round to the north and outflanked him again. Yet again he gave up the Rappahannock and fell back south of Warrenton, and, for the third time, Jackson outflanked him through Thoroughfare Gap, and at last got in his rear. Pope now had to fight; and the victory which perched upon our banners was the most brilliant of the war.

The participation of Jackson in the campaign of Maryland, and that of the Rappahannock, shared their glory, but without occasion for observation on those distinct and independent movements which were his *forte*, and for the display of which he had room in the Valley campaign, and that against Pope.

An incident occurred just upon the eve of the first battle before Fredericksburg, which is illustrative of his natural reticence—for he was habitually reserved and uncommunicative, never told his plans and never joked. On this occasion, however, he almost perpetrated a joke, and the recollection thereof will haunt the last survivor of those who were witnesses of the same. It was the narrowest escape he ever had. The battle was just about to break; indeed, it had already commenced, and Jackson sat intently surveying the field before him, when a young officer, ambling confidentially alongside, asked him, in the presence of several others now intensely interested, what his plans of attack or defence were; "for," said he, "if you should fall, General, it would be important that they should be known."

Jackson directly bent his body with a most gracious smile, and placing his hand to his mouth, and his mouth to the ear of the eager and now hugely gratified inquirer, asked in a whisper tolerably loud:

"Can you keep a secret?"

"Oh, most assuredly," was the answer.

To whom Jackson, in a louder voice and in tone perhaps a trifle triumphant, replied: "*And so can I!*" then, digging his spurs, cantered rapidly away, his keen grey eyes peering from under the slouched brim of his hat, and looking neither to the right nor the left—amid the uproarious laughter of the interested listeners, and the utter discomfiture of the man of inquiring mind.

At another time he is reported to have remarked, when questioned as to his plans:

"If my coat-tail knew what is in my head, I would cut it off."

He never failed to manifest his aversion to anything like inquisitiveness, and this habitual reticence was one of his strongest traits.

It was during the succeeding winter and the spring of 1863, that Jackson's private character, and especially the evidences of his piety, became known to the troops in camp. It was then that they learned to esteem him as a father. He was most assiduous in the revival work which was then progressing throughout the army of the Rappahannock, and especially in his own corps. That was a solemn and ever memorable season. Whole brigades were blessed by God's presence. Chaplains and missionaries united in preaching the word of life, and often the assemblage of soldiers was larger than could be gathered within reach of the speaker's voice (some two thousand or more), and of these, as many as five hundred, officers and men, might be seen pressing forward together to crave Divine favor in their behalf. The good work was wonderful, and at a time that might have been deemed anything but auspicious.

Among those who were prominent in these labors of Christian love among the soldiers, was the Rev. Dr. J. C. Stiles, a clergyman eminent in his profession, and universally beloved, and one of Jackson's warmest friends. He had passed nearly the whole winter in the camp of Jackson's corps, and from their daily intercourse and associations, the two had acquired for each other more than a fraternal regard. At length it became necessary that they should part, for the Doctor's duties called him to another field of labor. On the evening of his departure, he visited Jackson in his tent, where was had a most cordial interview, in the course of which the conversation turned upon a pamphlet which the Doctor had recently published upon the subject of "National Rectitude." Of this they talked much, and of kindred topics. When the Doctor took his hand to bid him farewell, Jackson said, "Well, Doctor—good bye! Now, you will do your part in preaching, and I'll do mine in fighting; and we will all pray, and the Lord will help us and make us a *righteous nation*. Remember, Doctor, you'll do your part—now, won't you?"

Was there ever such childlike simplicity? or a nobler representative of the church militant?

Jackson's regard for and strict observance of the Sabbath, is exemplified in the following extract of a letter to Col. A. R. Boteler:

"Guiney's Department, Caroline County, Va.,
"December 10, 1862.

"I have read with great interest the report of the Congressional Committee, recommending the repeal of the law requiring the mails to be carried on the Sabbath, and I hope that you will feel it a duty, as well as a pleasure, to urge its repeal. I do not see how a nation that thus arrays itself by such a law against God's holy day can expect to escape His wrath. The punishment of national sins must be confined to this world, as there are no nationalities beyond the grave. For fifteen years I have refused to mail letters on Sunday, or to take them out of the office on that day, except since I came into the field; and, so far from having to regret my course, it has been a source of true enjoyment. I have never sustained loss in observing what God enjoins, and I am well satisfied that the law should be repealed at the earliest practicable moment. My rule is to let the Sabbath mails remain unopened unless they contain a dispatch; but dispatches are generally sent by couriers, or telegraph, or by some special messenger. I do not recollect a single instance of any special dispatch having reached me since the commencement of the war by the mails.

"If you desire the repeal of the law, I trust you will bring all your influence to bear in its accomplishment. Now is the time, it appears to me, to effect so desirable an object. I understand that not only is our President, but also most of our Colonels, and a majority of our Congressmen, are professing Christians. God has greatly blessed us, and I trust He will make us that people to whom God is the Lord. Let us look to God for an illustration in our history, that 'righteousness exalteth a nation, but sin is a reproach to any people.'

"Very truly, your friend,

"T. J. JACKSON.

"To Col. A. R. Boteler, Richmond, Va."

Another letter upon the same subject was addressed to Col. Preston of Virginia, as recently as April 27th, and, it is reasonable to suppose, was the last he ever wrote. A special interest, therefore, attaches to it. It runs as follows:

"Near Fredericksburg, April 27, 1863.

"Dear Colonel: I am much gratified to see that you are one of the delegates to the General Assembly of our church, and to write to express the hope that something may be accomplished by you at the meeting of that influential body towards repealing the law requiring our mails to be carried on the Christian Sabbath. Recently I received a letter from a member of Congress, expressing the hope that the House of Representatives would act upon the subject during the present session, and from the mention made of Col. Chilton and Mr Curry of Alabama, I infer that they are members of the committee which recommended the repeal of the law, though of this I am not certain. A few days since I received a very gratifying letter from Mr. Curry which was entirely voluntary on his part, as I was a stranger to him, and there had been no previous correspondence between us. His letter is of a cheering character, and he takes occasion to say that divine laws can be violated with impunity neither by governments nor individuals. I regret to say that he is fearful that the anxiety of members to return home, and the press of the business will prevent the desired action this session. I have said thus much in order that you may see that Congressional action is to be looked for next session, and hence the importance that Christians act promptly, so that our Legislature may see the current of public opinion before they take up the subject. I hope and pray that such may be our country's sentiment on this and kindred subjects, that our statesmen will see their way clear. Now appears to me an auspicious moment for action, as the people are looking to God for assistance.

"Very truly, your friend,

"T. J. JACKSON."

Every opinion of this great man, who has so recently given his life for his country, ought to have weight with his countrymen. At the late Presbyterian General Assembly a letter was read in which he gave, at the earnest solicitation of another, and through his modest appreciation of himself with evident reluctance, his opinion on the subject of providing religious instruction for the Army. We make some extracts. He says:

"My views are summed up in few words.

"Each branch of the Christian Church should send into the army some of its most prominent ministers who are distinguished for their piety, talents and zeal, and such ministers should labor to produce concert of action among chaplains and Christians in the army. These ministers should give special attention to preaching to regiments which are without chaplains, and induce them to take steps to get chaplains, to let the regiments name the denominations from which they desire chaplains selected, and then to see that suitable chaplains are secured. A bad selection of a chaplain may prove a curse instead of a blessing. If the few prominent ministers thus connected with each army would cordially co-operate, I believe that glorious fruits would be the result. Denominational distinctions should be kept out of view—and not touched upon. And, as a general rule, I do not think that a chaplain who would preach denominational sermons should be in the army. His congregation is his regiment, and it is composed of various denominations. I would like to see no question asked in the army what denomination a chaplain belongs to, but let the question be, does he preach the Gospel? The neglect of the spiritual interests of the army may be seen from the fact that not one half of my regiments have chaplains. * * * * * *

"Among the wants of the Church in the army, is some ministers of such acknowledged superiority and zeal, as under God, to be the means of giving concert of action. Our chaplains, at least in the same military organization encamped in the same neighborhood, should have their meetings, and through God's blessing devise successful plans for spiritual conquests. All the other departments of the army have system, and such system exists in any other department of the service, that no one of its officers can neglect his duty without diminishing the efficiency of his branch of the service. And it appears to me that when men see what attention is bestowed secularly in comparison with what is religiously, they naturally under-estimate the importance of religion. From what I have said, you may think I am despondent; but thanks to an ever kind Providence, such is not the case. I do not know when so many men brought together without any religious test, exhibit so much religious feeling.

"The striking feature is that so much that is hopeful should exist, when so little human instrumentality has been employed for its accomplishment. In civil life ministers have regular meetings to devise means for co-operation in advancing the interests of the Church. This can be done in the army, and I am persuaded it should be. * * * * * * * *

"Some ministers ask for leave of absence for such trivial objects in comparison with the salvation of the soul that I fear they give occasion to others to think that such ministers do not believe that the salvation of the soul is as important as they preach. It is the special province of the chaplains to look after the spiritual interests of the army, and I greatly desire to see them evincing a rational zeal proportional to the importance of their mission. Do not believe that I think the chaplains are the only delinquents. I do not believe, but know, that I am a great delinquent, and I not only design saying what I have said respecting the laxness of chaplains to apply to all of them. I would like to see each Christian denomination send one of its great lights into the army. By this arrangement I trust that if any one should have denominational feelings that they will not be in the way of advancing a common and glorious cause."

Jackson evidently lived by faith, and conquered by prayer. It was said of him, that when he was not fighting he was generally praying. Visitors to his quarters often complained because it took him so long to conclude his devotions, and they meanwhile waiting patiently without. At all times and seasons he seemed to recognize the presence of God, and to be invoking the Divine aid, whether in the midnight hour of the silent camp, in the thunder and tumult of the battle-field, or in his solitary forest strolls by day. It is well authenticated that he always sought especial aid through prayer on the eve of a conflict, and the published saying of his negro servant is vouched for as correct: "When Mars'r get up two or tree times in de night to pray, den I knows dat somefin's comin' next day. Bress de Lor!" He was frequently observed to hold up his left hand in battle, apparently unconscious of all that was transpiring around him, and he was generally believed to be then engaged in prayer. Once, while so occupied, his hand was struck by a flying bullet, but he neither winced nor lowered his hand until his devotions were concluded.

It is not at all remarkable that his troops should have been animated with the spirit, bravery, and confidence of such a leader. There is something mysterious and awe-inspiring in this invisible communication between the spiritual and material world, this silent acknowledgment of the Divine essence pervading all things and the strange immunity from harm which the faith of the subject seems to weave around him. The time, the occasion, and the individual, beget a sympathy of feeling in the hearts of his followers, and some unappreciable, magnetic influence draws them on where the spirit of inspiration leads. Men, under such circumstances, become superhuman. Both their mental and physical organism undergoes a change. Are we surprised that they thought that Jackson bore a charmed life, or that, like Achilles, he was actually invulnerable from head to heel! The true secret of his conduct was that he had dedicated his soul to God, and his life unreservedly to the service of his country and the establishment of her liberties, and feared not death, nor quailed where the post of danger was the post of duty.

Another instance of his devotion to the cause he had at heart is recorded in a published letter, the writer of which made a parting call upon him in his tent, upon the banks of the Rappahannock. "As we stood exchanging last words (the letter reads), some reference was made to what our ladies are doing. "Yes,' said he, 'but they must not entice the men away from the army. You may tell them so for me. *We are fighting for principle, for honor, for everythiny we hold dear. If we fall, we lose everything. We shall then be slaves—we shall be worse than slaves—we shall have nothing worth living for.'*

"I am sure the women of the Confederacy will give these words of the now lamented hero a place in their hearts. Let them not be impatient even about their friends in the army coming on visits home. Let them encourage and cheer them in staying at their posts whenever and so long as may be necessary.

"But, whether there may have been such occasion for such a suggestion to them or not, the words which Jackson spoke in connection with it, are words alike noble and solemn, to which every man, as well as woman in the Confederate States ought to listen. Let our soldiers inscribe them on their banners. Let our citizens at home keep them before their eyes. Let those who are mad in the pursuit of gain, amid the sufferings of their country, and their fellow-citizens give ear to the tones of the warning which these words convey!"

To the casual observer there was nothing striking in the form or face of Jackson. In citizen's dress, he might have been taken for a plain farmer, of perhaps more than ordinary intelligence. But those who could see nothing great in him hold to the stage idea of a hero. The physiognomist would have looked twice, and a close scrutiny would have convinced him that a man of no ordinary abilities was before him. He was a muscular man, six feet high, with clear white complexion, blueish grey eyes, sharp nose, and a prominent chin set on a powerful and well-curved jaw. His skull was magnificent in size and shape, the forehead both broad and high, and balanced by a long, deep mass behind and above the ear. Many are the newspaper descriptions of his personal appearance, but we prefer to give here the impartial testimony of a stranger—an Englishman, who visited him at his headquarters near Martinsburg last year, and has transmitted to Blackwood's Magazine the fruits of his observations. The narrator says :

"With him we spent a most pleasant hour, and were agreeably surprised to find him very affable, having been led to expect that he was silent and almost morose. Dressed in his grey uniform, he looks the hero that he is; and his thin, compressed lips and calm glance, which meets yours unflinchingly, give evidence of that firmness and decision of character for which he is so famous. He has a broad, open forehead, from which the hair is well brushed back; a shapely nose, straight and rather long; thin colorless cheeks, with only a very small allowance of whiskers; a cleanly shaven upper lip and chin, and fine greyish blue eyes, rather sunken with overhanging brows, which intensify the keenness of his gaze, but without imparting fierceness to it. Such are the general characteristics of his face, and I have only to add that a smile seems always lurking about his mouth when he speaks, and that, though his voice partakes slightly of that harshness which Europeans unjustly attribute to all Americans, there is much unmistakable cordiality in his manner; and to us he talked most affectionately of England and of his brief but enjoyable sojourn there. The religious element seems strongly developed in him, and, though his conversation is perfectly free from all puritanical cant, it is evident that he is a person who never loses sight of the fact that there is an omnipresent Deity ever presiding over the minutest occurrences of life as well as over the most important. Altogether, as one of his soldiers said to me in talking, "he is a glorious fellow!" and after I left him I felt that I had at last solved the mystery of "Stonewall Brigade," and discovered why it was that it had accomplished such almost miraculous feats. With such a leader men would go anywhere and face any amount of difficulties, and, for myself, I believe that, inspired by the presence of such a man, I should be perfectly insensible to fatigue, and reckon upon success as a moral certainty. While Gen. Lee is regarded in the light of infallible Jove, a man to be reverenced, Jackson is loved and adored with all that childlike and trustful affection which the ancients are said to have lavished upon the particular deity presiding over their affairs. The feeling of the soldiers of General Lee resembles that which Wellington's troops entertained for him—namely, a fixed and unshaken faith in all he did, and a calm confidence of victory when serving under him. But Jackson, like Napoleon, is idolized with that intense fervor, which, consisting of mingled personal attachment and devoted loyalty, caused them to meet death for his sake and bless him when dying."

This is certainly a high tribute to the character and estimable worth of the heroic individual whose loss the nation has now to mourn, and the more to be prized in consideration of its source. His name has already become a synomym of true greatness, and there is none that will more readily command the eulogium of the civilized world. The nations will vie to do him honor.

We come now to the last of his great services in his country's cause. A few nights before the great battle, he was discussing with one of his aids the probability and issue of a battle, when he became unusually excited. After talking it over fully, he paused and with deep humility and reverence said, "My trust is in God," then as if the sound of battle was in his ear, he raised himself to his tallest stature, and with flashing eyes and a face all blazoned with the fire of the conflict, he exclaimed, "I wish they would come." This humble trust in God, combined with the spirit of the war-horse whose neck is "clothed with thunder," and who "smelleth the battle afar off, the thunder of the captains and the shouting," made that rare and lofty type of martial prowess that has shrined Jackson among the great heroes of the world. Trust in God and eagerness for the fray were two of the great elements of that marvellous success that seemed to follow him like a star, so that he was never defeated, or failed in any thing he undertook.

The enemy *did* come at last, and they came in overwhelming hosts, such as the history of wars has seldom recorded for numbers, threatening the annihilation of the Spartan band that were summoned to oppose them. For a while victory seemed to ride upon their advancing banners, and they became so confident of success, that they telegraphed to Washington that the triumph of the Federal arms was assured. But Lee, and Jackson, and Hill, and other brave spirits who did not know defeat, were there to contest the field. When the conflict was at its height, Jackson was selected, as usual, to operate upon the enemy's flank and rear. Lee asked him if he could do it by starting at three in the morning? "I can do it if you let me start now," was the reply. "Use your own discretion," said Lee; and away old Stonewall flew. This was on Friday evening. And his movement was swifter even than Lee contemplated. Gen. Hooker had occupied Saturday in awaiting the Confederate attack, which was evidently expected in front. The movements of the enemy seemed to indicate that they were retreating, and as the main line of their retreat was occupied by our forces, an attack to recover that line was confidently expected. What was the surprise, then, to find Stonewall Jackson, on Saturday afternoon, upon our extreme right and rear, between Chancellorsville and Germania Mills?

No words can convey the faintest impression of the enthusiasm and confidence, that swift as the electric current brightened each face, as the news spread from man to man on our long line, "Old Stonewall's come; Jackson's here, boys!" and the next moment he emerged from the timber on the hill two hundred yards away, and came dashing furiously on. But two of his staff were with him, one of whom rode ten or fifteen steps behind, the other an equal distance further back; all spurred their horses to their utmost speed. Hundreds of hats were flying in the air, and wild shouts from the troops, as he literally flew onward. He held his own hat in his left hand, giving it a flourish over his head occasionally, and kept continually turning his face first to the right, then the left, and presently disappeared over the crest of a hill in front. His presenee was soon practically felt by every one of the troops. Under his lead they abandoned their fortifications, and started forward in quiek time to attack the enemy, instead of waiting for his onset. As they filed down the road, the great General rode along the lines, his elear gray eyes beaming with the ardor of the patriot soldier, and his whole face radiant in the prospect of once more hurling destruetion and havoc in the serried ranks of his country's invaders.

Gen. Hooker's plan was to make a feint in strong force a little below Frederieksburg, as though he intended to give battle on the field of December 13th, while he moved his main force higher up, and crossed the river at points about opposite Chancellorsville, which is situated on the plank road leading from Fredericksburg to Orange Court House, twelve miles from the former plaee; and then by moving out from the river, and towards Spottsylvania Court House and Guinea's Station, occupy a position on the flank in the rear of Gen. Lee.

Gen. Lee, either knowing or correctly anticipating a movement of this kind, withdrew the whole of his force (except Gen. Early's division and Barksdale's brigade, which were left to defend the crossings at and below Frederieksburg) and marehed along the Orange Court House plank road to meet the enemy. As soon as Gen. Hooker became aware of this movement knowing that a battle in that neighborhood would be inevitable, he took position above and below Chancellorsville, and intrenehed himself on both sides of the road, his works being at right angles to the road, and facing towards Fredericksburg. When within two or three miles of Chaneellorsville, Gen. Lee eame upon the enemy. Here he plaeed the divisions of Gens. McLaws and Anderson in position, while Gen. Jackson with his eorps was ordered up the Catarpin road, leaving the plank road on his right. After passing up that road until he reached a point above the position of the enemy he turned to the right, and fell into the plank road about two miles above Chancellorsville, and immediately behind the enemy's entrenehments. This movement took the Yankees eompletely by surprise. McLaws and Anderson fought them in front and extended their line to the left, while Stonewall eame down like a terrible tornado upon his rear, at the same time extending his right until the two wings of our army met upon the flank of the enemy, who were driven in wild eonfusion from their position on the road, and compelled to fall back between that and the river.

Our right and left wings were then extended until our lines reached from the river below Chancellorsville, to the river above, thus occupying three sides of Hooker's position. Our line of battle then formed a V with the apex resting on the plank road at Chancellorsville, and the enemy between that and the river, a distance of five miles or thereabouts.

Never was a more daring movement attempted and so brilliantly carried out; never an enemy so completely out-generaled. From being the flanking party, he suddenly found himself not only flanked, but a strong and terrible force in the rear of his entrenchments. His prospects at this time were gloomy and desperate in the extreme, while ours were indeed glorious, and would doubtless have been realized to the satisfaction of the most sanguine, but that Gen. Early, by some (as yet) unexplained means, allowed the enemy to cross at Fredericksburg and force him from his strong position and to advance three miles up the plank road. In consequence of this it became necessary for Gen. Lee to withdraw Gen. McLaws' and a part of Gen. Anderson's division from the attack and send them down the road to drive the enemy back to Fredericksburg and across the river. The result was that the pursuit of the flying enemy had to be temporarily abandoned, and Hooker, taking advantage of this opportunity, so strengthened his position on the river, and on the hills beyond, as to enable him to make his escape. If Gen. Early had held his strong position, Gen. Lee would have completely destroyed Hooker's army. There is no telling what the grand results would have been.

Jackson surpassed himself in that day's fight; but alas! that great work was his last! The sad calamity which was to call forth the tears of the nation and drape every heart in mourning was about to fall with its crushing weight of bereavement. We shrink from the painful duty which is demanded of the memorialist.

After the close of the fighting on Saturday night, Gen. Jackson, in company with a number of his own and a part of the staff of A. P. Hill, had ridden beyond the front line of skirmishers, as was often his wont. When he had finished his observations, and was returning, about 8 o'clock, the cavalcade was, in the darkness of the night, mistaken for a body of the enemy's cavalry and fired upon by a regiment of his own corps. He was struck by three balls: one through the left arm, two inches below the shoulder joint, shattering the bone and severing the chief artery; another ball passed through the same arm, between the elbow and wrist, making its exit through the palm of the hand; a third ball entered the palm of the right hand about its middle, and passing through, broke two of the bones. He fell from his horse and was caught by Captain Wormley, to whom he remarked: "All my wounds are by my own men." He had given orders to fire at anything coming up the road before he left the lines. The enemy's skirmishers appeared ahead of him and he turned to ride back. Just then, some one cried out, "cavalry!" "charge!" and immediately the regiment area. The whole party broke forward to ride through our line to escape the fire. Capt. Boswell was killed and carried through the line by his horse and fell amid our own men. Col. Crutchfield, Chief of Staff, was wounded by his side. Two couriers were killed. Major Pendleton, Lieutenants Morrison and Smith, aids, escaped uninjured.

Gen. Jackson was immediately placed on a litter and started for the rear; the firing attracted the attention of the enemy, and was resumed by both lines. One of the litter bearers was shot down, and the General fell from the shoulders of the men, receiving a severe contusion, which added to the injury of the arm and injuring the side severely. The enemy's fire of artillery on the point was terrible. General Jackson was left for five minutes until the fire slackened, then placed in an ambulance and carried to the field hospital at Wilderness Run. He lost a large amount of blood, and at one time told Dr. McGuire he thought he was dying, and would have bled to death, but a tourniquet was immediately applied. For two hours he was near pulseless from the shock. As he was being carried from the field, frequent enquiries were made by the soldiers, "Who have you there?" He told the Doctor, "Do not tell the troops I am wounded." He seemed to retain his usual cheerfulness.

Conversing with an aid, he pointed to his mutilated arm and said, "Many people would regard this as a great misfortune; I regard it as one of the greatest blessings of my life." Mr. S. remarked. "All things work together for good, to those that love God." "Yes, yes," he emphatically said, "that's it, that's it."

After reaction a consultation was held between Drs. Black, Coleman, Walls and McGuire, and amputation was decided upon. He was asked, "If we find amputation necessary shall it be done at once?" He replied, "Yes! certainly, Dr. McGuire, do for me whatever you think right." The operation was performed while under the influence of chloroform, and was borne well. Once during the amputation he swooned, and was for some minutes unconscious. When he had partially recovered, some one asked him how he felt. He replied cheerfully, "Very comfortable," then paused for an instant, as though recalling suddenly something forgotten; and with kindling eye and lips compressed, spoke out in the firm sharp tone of command: "Order forward the infantry to the front!"

Noble man! it was not a passing vagary of delirium, but rather a momentary forgetfulness of self, his situation and his wounds, and an anxious concern for the charge that had been entrusted to him. Presently he remarked to a friend the pleasurableness of the sensations in taking chloroform; stating that he was conscious of every thing that was done to him, that the sawing of his bone sounded to him like the sweetest music, and every sensation was one of delight.

Meanwhile a messenger had been despatched to Gen. Lee with the intelligence of this severe misfortune. It was about 4 o'clock on Sunday morning. The General was found asleep upon a pallet of straw, where he had sought rest during the short respite from battle that the interval of night afforded. When informed of what had occurred, he said fervently: "Thank God, it is no worse; God be praised that he is still alive," then added, "Any victory is a dear one that deprives us of the services of Jackson, even for a short time."

Upon the informant mentioning that he believed it was General Jackson's intention to have pressed them on Sunday had he not have fallen, General Lee quietly said: "These people shall be pressed to-day," at the same time rising. Hastily dressing and partaking of his simple fare of ham and cracker, he sallied forth, unattended, and made such dispositions as rendered the Sabbath a blessed day for onr cause, even though a Jackson had fallen among its leaders.

The letter of Lee to Jackson, so full of characteristic generosity and heartfelt sorrow for his friend, is worthy the highest place among the memorials of great men. "Greater love hath no man than this, that he lay down his life for his friend."

CHANCELLORSVILLE, May 4th.

General—I have just received your note informing me that you were wounded. I cannot express my regret at the occurrence. Could I have dictated events, I should have chosen for the good of the country to have been disabled in your stead.

I congratulate you upon the victory which is due to your skill and energy.

Most truly yours, R. E. LEE.

Jackson heard the letter read, and with manifest emotion. His reply was noble, and just what might have been expected of him. With his usual modesty and reverence, he said: "General Lee should give the glory to God." He always seemed jealous of the glory of his Saviour. Then, bursting into tears, he exclaimed, "far better for the Confederacy that ten Jacksons had fallen than one Lee!"

Another touching evidence of General Lee's appreciation of Jackson was afforded when Mrs. Jackson reached his headquarters in search of her wounded husband. She is said to have remarked, upon entering:

"I am told that Gen. Jackson has lost his left arm."

"Yes, madam," was Gen. Lee's reply; "and I have lost my right."

Par nobile fratrum! What reciprocity of esteem! The loves of Damon and Pythias are more than rivalled by those of these twin heroes in arms—these soldiers of the church militant. Patriotism is exalted in the lives and death of such good men.

On Sunday morning Jackson slept well, was cheerful, and his condition every way encouraging. He sent for Mrs. Jackson and asked minutely about the battle, spoke cheerfully of the result, and said, "If I had not been wounded, or had had an hour more of daylight, I would have cut off the enemy from the road to the U. S. Ford, and we would have had them entirely surrounded and they would have been obliged to surrender, or cut their way out; they had no other alternative. My troops may sometimes fail in driving the enemy from a position, but the enemy always fail to drive my men from a position." This was said smilingly.

When it was told him that Gen. Stuart led his old Stonewall Brigade to the charge with the watchword; "charge, and remember Jackson," and that inspired by this they made so brilliant and resistless an onset, he was deeply moved, and said, "it was just like them; it was just like them. They are a noble body of men." He was deeply affected by Gen. Paxton's death.

In the afternoon he complained of the fall from the litter, although no contusion or abrasion was perceptible as the result of the fall; he did not complain of his wounds—never spoke of them unless asked.

On Sunday evening he slept well.

On Monday he was carried to Chancellors' House, near Guinea's Depot; he was cheerful, talked about the battle, the gallant bearing of Gen. Rhodes, and said that his Major General's commission ought to date from Saturday; of the grand charge of his old Stonewall Brigade, of which he had heard; asked after all his officers; during the day talked more than usual, and said: "The men who live through this war will be proud to say, I was one of the Stonewall Brigade to their children." He insisted that the term "Stonewall" belonged to them and not to him.

During the ride to Guinea's he complained greatly of heat, and besides wet applications to the wound, begged that a wet cloth be applied to his stomach, which was done, greatly to his relief, as he expressed it. He slept well Monday night, and ate with relish on next morning.

Tuesday—his wounds were doing very well. He asked, "can you tell me from the appearance of my wounds, how long I will be kept from the field." He was greatly satisfied when told they were doing remarkably well. Did not complain of any pain in his side, and wanted to see the members of his staff, but was advised not.

Wednesday—The wounds looked remarkably well. He expected to go to Richmond this day, but was prevented by the rain. This night, whilst his surgeon, who had slept none for three nights, was asleep, he complained of nausea, and ordered his boy, Jim, to place a wet towel over his stomach. This was done. About daylight the surgeon was awakened by the boy saying, the General is suffering great pain. The pain was in the right side, and due to incipient pneumonia and some nervousness, which he himself attributed to the fall from the litter.

That pneumonia was the immediate cause of his death, and was contracted on the night preceding that on which he received his wounds, through his unselfish anxiety for the health of a young member of his staff. They were in the open air, without tents, and having no extra covering at all, after great urgency he accepted the cape of one of his aids. In the night, however, when all were wrapped in deep sleep, Jackson arose, and gently laying the covering over the young aid, he laid down again and slept without any protection whatever. In the morning he awoke with a cold which ended in pneumonia.

Inexplicable dispensation of Providence! that he should have been not only shot down by the bullets of his friends, but that his very love for them should have turned to his own detriment and death. Truly, he laid down his life for his men. But it was so predestined. He had fulfilled his great purpose in history, and wrought out the mission for which he was ordained of Providence. "Dying, he left no stain which, living, he would wish to blot."

Thursday—Mrs. Jackson arrived, greatly to his joy and satisfaction, and she faithfully nursed him to the end. He continued hopeful, and endeavored to cheer those who were around him.

His mind ran very much on the Bible and religious topics. He enquired of Lieutenant S., a Theological student on his staff, whether they had ever debated in the Seminary the question, whether those who were miraculously cured by Jesus ever had a return of the disease. "I do not think," he said, "they could have returned, for the power was too great. The poor paralytic would never again shake with palsy. Oh! for infinite power!"

By evening of that day all pain had ceased. He suffered greatly from prostration. On Friday he suffered no pain, but the prostration increased.

Sunday morning, when it was apparent that he was rapidly sinking, Mrs. Jackson was informed of his condition. Noticing the sadness of his beloved wife, he said to her tenderly, "I know you would gladly give your life for me, but I am perfectly resigned. Do not be sad—I hope I shall recover. Pray for me but always remember in your prayer to use the petition, thy will be done." Those who were around him noticed a remarkable development of tenderness in his manner and feelings during his illness, that was a beautiful mellowing of that iron sternness and impurturbable calm that characterized him in his military operations. Advising his wife, in the event of his death, to return to her father's house, he remarked, "You have a kind and good father. But there is no one so kind and good as your Heavenly Father." When she told him that the doctors did not think he could live two hours, although he did not himself expect to die, he replied, "It will be infinite gain to be translated to Heaven, and be with Jesus. It is all right." He had previously said, "I consider these wounds a blessing; they were given me for some good and wise purpose, and I would not part with them if I could." He then said he had much to say to her, but was too weak. At one time he was offered stimulants to prolong his existence, but these he refused to take. Shortly after his mind began to wander. He had always desired to die, if it were God's will, on the Sabbath, and seemed to greet its light that day with peculiar pleasure, saying, with evident delight, "it is the Lord's day," and enquired anxiously what provision had been made for preaching to the army; and having ascertained that arrangements were made, he was contented. Delirium, which occasionally manifested itself during the last two days, prevented some of the utterances of his faith which would doubtless have otherwise been made. His thoughts vibrated between religious subjects and the battle-field, now asking some question about the Bible, or church history, and then giving an order, "Pass the infantry to the front," "Tell Major Hawks to send forward provisions to the men," "A. P Hill, prepare for action," "Let us cross over the river, and rest under the shade of the trees," until at last, amid the full recognition of the hand of God in his destiny, at a quarter past three o'clock, his gallant spirit gently passed over the dark river, and entered on its rest where the tree of life is blooming beside the crystal river in the better country

Thus passed away the high-souled, heroic man, falling like Sidney and Hampden in the beginning of the struggle to which his life was devoted, bequeathing to those who survive him a name and memory, that under God may compensate for his early, and to us apparently untimely fall. A little child of the family, when the hero was dying, was taunted with Jackson's wound by some of the prisoners who were collected there awaiting transportation. "We have a hundred Jacksons left if he does die," was the heroic reply of the child. And so we trust it will be. The spirit of Jackson will be breathed into a thousand hearts which will emulate his bravery, and seek to make up for his loss, and in the end his memory and glory, his holy life, his manly piety, and his glorious death may be a richer blessing to us than if his life had been spared. His high religious character, his courage, skill, rapidity of motion, and marvellous success, had given him a hold on the army such as no other man had, and it was felt that his very name was a symbol of victory. There was no man who inspired the enemy with so much terror, or for whom they had in their secret heart a more unbounded respect. He has shown the way to victory, and we trust that many a gallant spirit will come forward eagerly to tread it, and that our dead hero shall be worth to us more than a host of living ones. It will be if we copy his piety as well as his bravery, and like him, cherish the feeling that he so strikingly expressed as he paced his tent before the battle. "My trust is in God—I wish they would come on."

The age of Gen. Jackson, as given on the silver plate of his coffin, is as follows: Lieutenant-General Thomas J. Jackson.—Born January 21st, 1824; died May 10th, 1863. He was, therefore, a little above 39 years of age. A few days before the battle of

Chancellorsville his photograph was successfully taken. Galt had just before his death, secured a *bas relief*, and Volk, while Jackson's body was lying in state at the Governor's mansion, took a cast which is said, by those who have seen it, to be a perfect *fac simile*.

Gen. Jackson was twice married. The first time to a daughter of Rev. Dr. Junkin. Her children all died. His widow was Miss Morrison, of North Carolina, and, with an infant daughter of six months, now survives him.

The announcement of his death spread a gloom over the whole country. It was a bitter disappointment; for the people, knowing the nature of his wounds, had fondly promised themselves that his invaluable services would soon be restored to the Republic. They hoped that he might live to enjoy in an honorable peace the reward of his toils and dangers in the camp. But an all-wise Providence decreed differently, and the country must bow reverently before the decision of the Omnipotent One. A painful interest attaches to the order of Gen. Lee, announcing to the army their great bereavement.

Headquarters, Army Northern Va.,
May 11, 1863.

General Orders, No. 61.

With deep grief the commanding General announces to the army the death of Lieut. Gen. T. J. Jackson, who expired on the 10th inst., at 3¼ p. m. The daring, skill and energy of this great and good soldier, by the decrees of an all-wise Providence, are now lost to us. But while we mourn his death, we feel that his spirit still lives, and will inspire the whole army with his indomitable courage and unshaken confidence in God as our hope and our strength. Let his name be a watchword to his corps, who have followed him to victory on so many fields. Let officers and soldiers emulate his invincible determination to do everything in the defence of our beloved country.

R. E. LEE, General.

THE OBSEQUIES.

At 4 o'clock, on the afternoon of the 11th of May, the mortal remains of Jackson were received in Richmond from Guinea's Depot, in Caroline county.

The announcement that they would arrive at 12 o'clock caused an entire suspension of business, and a turn out at the depot of nearly all the inhabitants of the city, who were anxious to pay the last tribute of respect to the departed chieftain. When it was known that the body would not reach the city before 4 o'clock, the immense crowd slowly dispersed, but assembled again at the last hour indicated in even greater force than before. The tolling of the different bells gave the signal that the cars were slowly wending their way down Broad street, when preparations were made for the reception of the body by an appropriate disposition of the military.

The train was stopped at the corner of 4th and Broad streets, and after a short delay the coffin containing the body was removed to the hearse in attendance. It was enveloped in the *new* flag of the Confederacy, and the first use that was ever made of it was thus to enwrap the remains of the departed chieftain. This circumstance alone is sufficient to consecrate the newly adopted banner in the hearts of the people. On the flag were placed wreaths of evergreen and rare flowers. A few minutes before five o'clock Gen. Elzy gave the command and the procession started.

The procession (the military with reversed arms) marched slowly to the corner of Ninth street, and turned toward Main, entering the Capitol Square by the gate on Grace street. The military having formed a line extending across the Square past Washington's monument, the body was slowly conveyed down the line to the Governor's mansion, and carried into the large reception room. The bells were tolled till sundown, till which time hundreds of people remained on the Square. Never before was such a heartfelt and general manifestation of grief in Richmond, at any event, as was then and there enacted.

The following day the body was transferred from the Governor's House to the Capitol. At noon a long procession passed through the streets of the city. The arms of the soldiers were reversed, their banners were draped in mourning. The drums were muffled and the notes of trumpet and horn were funereal. The tolling bell and the cannon booming at long intervals, told a mournful story.

The war-worn veterans of Picket's division were there. Ewell, brave, modest and maimed, rode close to the hearse of his great commander. The President of the Confederate States, pale and sorrowful, was there. The good Governor of Virginia, stricken with grief for the loss of the noble townsman, was there. The Heads of Departments, the State and Metropolitan Authorities, and many citizens, walked humbly and sadly behind the coffin, decked with spring flowers and enveloped in the folds of a flag which the nations of the earth have never beheld. And they were silent as before. All was hushed while the mortal remains of the best and best beloved chieftain in all the land passed onward to the Capitol of the State and the Confederacy, which he had so heroically defended and died to save from pollution. The body of Stonewall Jackson was in the hearse, and this great procession was in his honor.

It was under the charge of Gen. George W. Randolph, as Chief Marshal, and consisted of the following civil and military bodies:

The Public Guard, with Armory Band, followed by the 19th and 56th Virginia Infantry, Major Wren's Battalion of Cavalry, and the Richmond Lafayette Artillery, all preceded by a full band; the hearse, drawn by four white horses, appropriately caparisoned, the hearse draped and plumed, and the coffin wrapped in the Confederate flag and decorated with flowers; the pall-bearers, consisting of the staff of the lamented hero, and several other officers of high rank, wearing the insignia of mourning; carriages containing first his Excellency, the President, and the family of the deceased, followed by personal friends and distinguished admirers; the various Chiefs of Departments, State and Confederate, civil, military and judicial; the Governor of the State, attended by his aids; the Mayor of the city and Members of the Council.

On either side and in the rear an immense throng of ladies and gentlemen, children, servants and soldiers mingled, ready to move along with the procession. The banners were draped with crape, the swords of the military officials were draped at the hilt; the cannon of the artillery wore the sad insignia, the arms of the infantry were reversed, the drums were muffled, and at the given hour a gun stationed beneath the monument, boomed forth the signal for motion. The streets were crowded with people, the stores were closed as the pageant moved along, and from many windows and balconies floated flags, draped in mourning. The flags upon the public buildings remained, as on the day previous, at half-mast. The scene upon Main street was beyond adequate description, so impressive, so beautiful, so full of stirring associations, blending with the martial dirges of the bands, the gleam of the musket, rifle and sabre drawn, the sheen of the black cannon, the thousands of throbbing hearts, and the soul of sorrow that mantled over all.

From Second street, through which the procession partly passed, it wheeled into Grace street, down which it returned to the Capitol square, entering the Monument gate. At different stages of the obsequies the cannon which remained stationed at the foot of the Monument, pealed out a tone of thunder, which heightened the effect of the tolling bells, the solemn music and the grand display. The hearse being drawn up in front of the Capitol, the coffin was removed to the hall of the House of Representatives, where it was laid in state in front of the Speaker's seat. Thousands crowded into the building, many bearing splendid boquets with which to adorn the coffin. One look, though it sufficed not, was all that could be obtained by each visitor, the throng behind pressing each visitor forward; the features of the mighty warrior in death's repose, graven upon and borne away upon the tablets of the memory of all. Children of tender years, maiden and youth, who had never seen "Stonewall" Jackson living, crowded in full of the parental injunction to look upon the features of "Stonewall" Jackson dead. What a memory these youthful minds bore away, to be recalled when their children's children speak of him in after years. It was estimated that fully twenty thousand persons viewed the body.

The face of the dead displayed the same indomitable lines of firmness, with the long, slightly acquiline nose, and high forehead of marble whiteness, but the cheeks presented a deep palor. The eyelids were firmly closed, the mouth natural, and the whole contour of the face composed, the full beard and moustache remaining. The body was dressed in a full citizen's suit, it being the object of his friends to preserve the uniform in which he fought and fell. The doors of the Hall were kept open to visitors until nine o'clock in the evening, when they were closed, and Richmond took her farewell of "Stonewall" Jackson.

It was the last wish of the dying hero that he should be buried in Lexington, in the Valley of Virginia, amid the scenes familiar to his eyes through the years of his manhood, obscure and unrecorded, but perhaps filled with recollections to him not less affecting than those connected with the brief but crowded period passed upon a grander stage. This desire, expressed at such a time, demanded unhesitating compliance, although many will regret that his remains could not have lain beside those of Tyler and Monroe, in the seeluded spot upon the brink of the James, which has been well selected as the place of national honor for the illustrious dead of Virginia. In accordance with this desire Jackson's body was removed to Lexington, where it arrived on the afternoon of Thursday, the 14th day of May. It was attended by the corps of cadets, under Gen. F. H. Smith, the professor of the Institute, and a large number of citizens, and escorted in solemn procession to the Institute barracks, where it was deposited in the old lecture room of the illustrious deceased. The room was just as he left it two years before, save it was heavily draped in mourning—not having been occupied since his absence. The hall which had so often echoed the voice of the modest and unknown professor, received back the laurel-crowned hero with the applause of the world and the benedictions of a nation resting upon him. It was a touching scene, and brought tears to many eyes when the body was deposited just in front of the favorite chair from which his lectures were delivered. Professors, students, visitors, all were deeply moved by the sad and solemn occasion, and gazed in mute sorrow on the affecting spectacle of the dead hero lying in his familiar lecture room. Guns were fired every half hour during the day in honor of the departed chieftain.

On Friday, religious services were held in the church in which he had delighted to worship God for ten years before the beginning of his late brilliant career. They were conducted by the Rev. Dr. White, the only pastor Gen. Jackson ever had after he became an avowed soldier of the Cross—a pastor whom he tenderly loved, and whose religious counsels he modestly sought, even in the midst of the most absorbing scenes through which he had passed during the last two years.*

A civic and military procession was afterwards formed, conspicuous in which were those officers and soldiers of the old Stonewall Brigade who happened at the time to be in the county. It awakened thrilling associations to see the shattered fragments of this famous Brigade assembled under the flag of the heroic Liberty Hall boys. The same flag which for some time was the Regimental standard of Jackson's old Fourth Regiment, and which that regiment carried in triumph over the bloody field of Manassas, on the ever-memorable 21st day of July.

Slowly and sadly moved the funeral procession—the body enveloped in the flag of his country and covered with flowers, and borne on a caisson of the Cadet Battery draped in mourning; and when the escort returned from its solemn duty, all that remained to earth of JACKSON had been deposited in the silent tomb where reposed the relics of his former wife and child.

"He sleeps his last sleep, he has fought his last battle,
No sound can awake him to glory again."

JACKSON *is no more!* In the words of his beloved companion in arms, Gen. Beauregard, "The illustrious soldier, Lieutenant Gen. Thomas J. Jackson is dead. The memory of his high worth, conspicuous virtues and momentous services will be treasured in the heart and excite the pride of this country to all time. His renown is already identified with our revolution; and even our enemy admits his unselfish devotion to our cause, and admires his eminent qualities."

Yea, truly, even his enemies were constrained to do him honor to praise his valor, and acknowledge his virtues. Not one dare

* See Appendix B.

after a breath of slander against him? While living, he won their admiration, and called forth many a hasty demonstration of their approval. It is a solemn fact that the 11,000 Federal prisoners captured at Harper's Ferry cheered him heartily when he presented himself. Now cold in death, they give him their verbal tributes, which we esteem as born not so much of generous emotions, as wrung from them by the demands of an exacting conscience!

"Jackson (says one Federal journalist), was the most brilliant rebel General developed by this war. From his coolness and sagacity, rapid movements and stubbornness in the fight, and his invariable good fortune, he resembled Napoleon in his early career, more than does any other General of modern times. Wherever Jackson appeared on any field, victory seems to have perched upon his banners. He was a universal favorite in the rebel armies, and popular even in our own."

Another says: "Stonewall Jackson was a great General, a brave soldier, a noble Christian, and a pure man. Every one who possesses the slightest particle of magnanimity must admire the qualities for which Stonewall Jackson was celebrated—his heroism, his bravery, his sublime devotion, his purity of character. He is not the first instance of a good man devoting himself to a bad cause."

Others sing praises in similar strain. But we pass them by. We care little for the emanations of such as these. To his old classmate and companion in arms (in Mexico,) we ascribe a more tender sentiment and higher motive. Says McClellan, the best of the Federal Generals:

"No one can help admiring a man like Jackson. He was sincere, and true, and valiant. Yet no one has disappointed me more than he has. Jackson was one of my classmates, and at College never promised to be the man he has proved himself. He was always very slow, and acquired a lesson only after great labor. And yet his determination was so great that he never gave any thing up until he succeeded. His character seems to have changed since, for he has exhibited a great celerity in all his movements, while in command of rebel forces. Lee is perhaps the most able commander the rebels have, and Jackson was their best executive officer."

We forbear to extend this hasty sketch of our country's idol—for idolized he was, and perhaps that is why he was taken from us; yet we cannot refrain from appending here the beautiful tribute to his memory with which some gifted pen has graced the pages of the *Charleston Courier*:

"A General whose fame has filled the world, whose martial achievements have placed his name high in the list of immortal conquerors, has gone to the grave in the midst of his days. And not only does the country lament the death of a soldier who has never lost a battle, who was always in the right place at the right time, and who never failed to smite the foe with a fierce and resistless might, but one, who, to the higher qualities of a military chieftain, added those traits and features that gave him a place in the innermost heart of the people. The skill, and valor, and earnestness with which he fought, elicited profound and universal admiration; the humility, purity and godliness that adorned his character as a man, made him an object of reverence and love. He wielded a trenchant blade, but that blade was sanctified with the breath of prayer, and he was not more at home on the field of blood than at the mercy seat.

"His splendid martial exploits are too fresh in the memory to justify the special mention of them. We remember with tearful admiration the magnificent achievements he performed, at a time when the country was depressed by a series of military disasters and the enemy were exulting over the expectation of speedy and complete success. Success, signal and glorious success, crowned every battle he fought, and every victory he won yielded results of the highest value to the sacred cause in which he imperilled his life.

"Of all the generals in the army of the Confederacy, none possessed, in a larger degree than the hero whose death we deplore, the ability of endearing himself to the officers and men under his command. No portion of our forces were required to do more and bear more, to encounter greater danger and endure more severe hardships and privations than the soldiers he led into battle; yet there is now no general in command who is more respected and admired and beloved than he was. His men were ever ready to march and labor and fight. It was enough for them to know that he required the service, and no matter what was its nature, the gallant soldiers of the noble chieftain rendered it with cheerful alacrity and hearty earnestness. They appreciated the rare character of the remarkable man. They perceived that he was actuated by the highest motives yielded by patriotism and Christianity, that he was as careless of his ease as he was of his life, and catching the inspiration of the same grand motives, and sustained by the same lofty sense of duty, they took pleasure in imitating the example of their fearless leader.

"And the feeling of enthusiastic admiration with which he inspired the soldiers immediately under his leadership, was shared in a large measure by every officer and private in the Army of the Potomac. His appearance was always greeted with bursts of applause, and no matter how worn and weary the champions of freedom, when the beloved chieftain was seen approaching the air was rent with deafening shouts. He was the idol of the army.

"And outside the army every lip delighted to praise him, and every heart did him honor. His brilliant exploits had so impressed the people with a sense of his distinguished abilities and transcendent worth, that they deemed it well nigh impossible that defeat could befall our army if Jackson's sword was there, made resistless by Jackson's prayers. And while every fresh success enhanced the lustre of fame, the victories he won were rejoiced over with a richer gush of joy, because they were accepted as manifest tokens of the gracious favor with which heaven regarded our cause. The country believed that the green and fragrant wreaths that encircled his brow were placed there by Him who knighted Jacob near the brook Jabbok and every victory he won was received as a declaration that as a Prince he had wrestled with God and had prevailed. These feelings of reverence and admiration and love, now find expression in the tears that agony forces from the heart, as the country looks down with troubled brow upon the face of the hero, pale and cold in death. Every one feels as though he had sustained a personal bereavement. The shadow of this terrible grief rests upon every heart. Every home and every heart is clothed in mourning. The country weeps. When Absalom fell his father poured out deep lamentations over his untimely end, and regretted that he had not died in the stead of his son, but there was no one beside the royal mourner who would have been willing to sacrifice his life to raise the unnatural culprit from the doom stern justice inflicted upon him. There is not a man worthy to take part in this terrific contest who would not have cheerfully poured out his life blood if his death could have been accepted in the stead of that glorious chieftain. In the agony of this overwhelming sorrow we exclaim, 'Would to God I had died for thee!'"

* * * * * * * *

And now, as we turn sorrowfully away from the shrine at which we have offered our simple tribute, we will leave thereon this beautiful *immortelle*—a myrtle wreath of poesy which the Lynchburg *Virginian* has lovingly twined in honor of the good man :

JACKSON!

Greatness is fallen! See, ye sons of earth,
The conqueror conquered, even in the birth
Of lofty victory, and wonder at the change!
But yester-eve his thoughts on fields did range;
His eye was 'rapt in blaze, and freedom slept
Secure within his bosom, where she'd crept
For greater safety in the dreadful hour,
When wrathful tyranny unchained its power,
And bade her choose between submission's shame,
And loss of country, honor, and of name.
Now beams no more the eye's heroic light;
No more the pulse beats with a stern delight;
No more the sword directs the march of war;
Closed is the ear to the deep sullen roar
Of mighty combat—to th' exulting shout
Of marshalled vict'ry on the heels of rout—
He who in battle showed a Cæsar's skill,

A Bayard's fearlessness, a Cromwell's will.
But who surpassed them all in this—that crowned
With laurels such as never yet have bound
With greater beauty the triumphant head,
Gave all the praise to God—the God who led
Old Israel's hosts, when Pharaoh hemmed their way,
Thro' the dark waters unto Canaan's day—
He, too, is fallen!.

Now the very breath
Of war seems hushed, astonished at the death,
Which its red hand has wrought upon the chief
Of all its daring spirits.

On the leaf
Where splendid actions and immortal names
Blend their rich colors in the midst of flames,
Behold in characters, which, like the lightnings run,
JACKSON, the hero, patriot, Christian, man!
Ages shall sing his praise: a nation weeps—
Behold, how still the spirit of the mighty sleeps!

THE END.

APPENDIX A.

THE STONEWALL BRIGADE.—The regiments that compose the "Stonewall Brigade" are the 2d, 4th, 5th, 27th, and 33d Virginia regiments of infantry. They alone won the name and are entitled to the honors.

The Stonewall Artillery consists of the Rockbridge Artillery, formerly Pendleton's Battery, and Carpenter's Battery, from Alleghany.

The members of the Stonewall Brigade were justly proud of their commander, and Jackson was equally jealous of the fame of his men. After his fatal wound, he often alluded to them in terms of honest pride and affection, both while conscious and in his moments of delirium. He insisted that the name of "Stonewall" belonged to them and not to him, and his dying wish was that they should be known and designated as the Stonewall Brigade. It is said that he frequently expressed the desire that Gen. R. S. Ewell should succeed to the command of the corps, an officer who enjoyed his fullest confidence. Be that as it may, this gentleman has since been promoted to fill the place of his lamented and illustrious predecessor, and on the 29th of May was duly installed, to the general satisfaction of the army. The following resolutions were adopted by the Brigade on the occasion of Jackson's death:

CAMP PAXTON, near Fredericksburg,
May 15th, 1863.

Whereas, it has pleased Almighty God, in the exercise of supreme, but unsearchable wisdom, to strike down, in the midst of his career of honor and usefulness, our glorious hero, Lieut. Gen. Jackson, the officers and men of this Brigade, which he formerly commanded, who have followed him through the trying scenes of this great struggle, and who, by the blessings of Providence, under his guidance, have been enabled to do some good in our country's cause; who loved and cherished him as a friend, honored him as a great and good man, laboring with hand and heart and mind for our present and future welfare; who obeyed and confided in him as a leader of consummate skill and unyielding fortitude, and who now mourn his loss, unite in the following tribute of respect to his memory:

Resolved 1. That, in the death of Lieutenant General Jackson, the world has lost one of its best and purest men—our country and the Church of God "a bright and shining light"—the army one of its boldest and most daring leaders, and this Brigade a firm and unwavering friend.

Resolved 2. That General Jackson has closed his noble career by a death worthy of his life, and that while we mourn for him, and feel that no other leader can be *to us* all that *he* has been, yet we are not cast down or dispirited, but even more determined to do our whole duty, and if need be, to give our lives for a cause made more sacred by the blood of our martyrs.

Resolved 3. That, in accordance with General Jackson's wish, and the desire of this Brigade to honor its first great commander, the Secretary of War be requested to order that it be known and designated as the "Stonewall Brigade;" and that, in thus formally adopting a title which is inseparably connected with his name and fame, we will strive to render ourselves more worthy of it, by emulating his virtues, and, like him, devote all our energies in the great work before us, of securing to our beloved country the blessings of peace and independence.

C. A. RONALD, President.

R. W. HUNTER, Secretary.

APPENDIX B.

The following papers explain the honors which were paid to the memor of General Jackson, at the Virginia Military Institute, where for ten yeai he filled a Professor's Chair :

ADJUTANT GENERAL'S OFFICE, VA.
May 11th, 1863.

Major-General F. H. Smith, Superintendent Virginia Military Institute :

Sir : By command of the Governor I have this day to perform the mos painful duty of my official life, in announcing to you, and through you t the Faculty and Cadets of the Virginia Military Institute—the death of th great and good, the heroic and illustrious Lieutenant General T. J. Jacksor at 16 minutes past 3 o'clock, yesterday afternoon.

The heavy bereavement, over which every true heart within the bound of the Confederacy mourns with inexpressible sorrow, must fall, if possi ble, with heavier force upon that noble State Institution to which he cam from the battle fields of Mexico, and where he gave to his native State th first years' service of his modest and unobtrusive, but public spirited an useful life. It would be a senseless waste of words to attempt a eulog upon this great among the greatest of the sons who have immortalize Virginia. To the corps of Cadets of the Virginia Military Institute, wha a legacy he has left; what an example of all that is good and great an true in the character of a Christian soldier!

The Governor directs that the highest funeral honors be paid to his memory, that the customary outward badges of mourning be worn by all th officers and cadets of the Institution.

By command.

W. H. RICHARDSON, Adjutant General.

HEADQUARTERS VIRGINIA MILITARY INSTITUTE,
May 13, 1863.

General Orders No. 80.

It is the painful duty of the Superintendent to announce to the officers and cadets of this Institution, the death of their late associate and professor, Lieutenant General Thomas J. Jackson. He died at Guinea's Station, Caroline county, Va., on the 10th instant, of pneumonia, after a short but violent illness, supervening upon the severe wounds received in the battle of Chancellorsville. A nation mourns the loss of Gen. Jackson. First in the hearts of the brave men he has so often led to victory, there is not a home in this Confederacy that will not feel the loss, and lament it as a great national calamity. But our loss is distinctive. He was peculiarly our own. He came to us in 1851, a Lieutenant and Brevet Major of Artillery, from the Army of the late United States, upon the unanimous appointment of the Board of Visitors, as Professor of Natural and Experimental Philosophy and Instructor of Artillery. Here he labored with scrupulous fidelity, for ten years, in the duties of these important offices. Here he became a Soldier of the Cross; and, as a humble, conscientious and useful Christian man, he established the character which he has developed into the world renowned Christian hero. On the 20th of April, 1861, upon the order of his Excellency, Governor Letcher, he left the Institute, in command of the Corps of Cadets, for Camp Lee, Richmond, for service in the defence of his State and country; and he has never known a day of rest, until called by the Divine command to cease from his labors.

The military career of Gen. Jackson fills the most brilliant and momentous page in the history of our country, and in the achievements of our arms, and he stands forth a colossal figure in this war for our independence.

His country now returns him to us—not as he was when he left us; his spirit has gone to God who gave it. His mutilated body comes back to us—to his home—to be laid by us in his tomb. Reverently and affectionately we will discharge this last solemn duty. And,

"Though his earthly sun is set;
His light shall linger round us yet,
Bright—radiant—blest."

Young gentlemen of the Corps of Cadets—The memory of General Jackson is precious to you. You know how faithfully, how conscientiously he discharged every duty. You know that he was emphatically a man of God, and that christian principle impressed every act of his life. You know how he sustained the honor of our arms, when he commanded at Harper's Ferry—how gallantly he repulsed Patterson at Hainesville—the invincible stand he made with his Stonewall Brigade at Manassas. You know the brilliant series of successes and victories which immortalized his Valley campaign—for many of you were under his standard at McDowell, and pursued the discomfitted Milroy and Schenck to Franklin. You know his rapid march to the Chickahominy—how he turned the flank of McClellan at Gaines' Mill—his subsequent victory over Pope at Cedar Mountain—the part he bore in the great victory at second Manassas—his investment and capture of Harper's Ferry—his rapid march and great conflict at Sharpsburg—and when his last conflict was passed, the tribute of the magnanimous Lee, who would gladly have suffered in his own person, could he, by that sacrifice, have saved Gen. Jackson, and to whom alone, under God, he gave the whole glory of the great victory at Chancellorsville. Surely, the Virginia Military Institute has a precious inheritance in the memory of Gen. Jackson.

His work is finished; God gave him to us and his country; He fitted him for his work, and when his work was done, He called him to Himself. Submission to the will of his Heavenly Father—it may be said of him, that while in every heart there may be some murmuring—his will was to do and suffer the will of God.

Reverence the memory of such a man as General Jackson; imitate his virtues, and here, over his lifeless remains, reverently dedicate your services and your life, if need be, in defence of that cause so dear to his heart—the cause for which he fought and bled—the cause in which he died.

Let the Cadets' battery, which he so long commanded, honor his memory by half-hour guns to morrow, from sunrise to sunset, under the direction of the commandant of the Cadets.

Let the flag of the State and Confederacy be hung at half-mast to-morrow.

Let his Lecture Room be draped in mourning for the period of six months.

Let the Officers and Cadets of the Institute wear the usual badge of mourning for the period of thirty days; and it is respectfully requested that the Alumni of the Institution unite in this tribute of respect to the memory of their late Professor.

All duties will be suspended to-morrow.

By command of Major-General F. H. Smith,

(Signed) A. GOVAN HILL, A. A. V. M. I.

www.ingramcontent.com/pod-product-compliance
Lightning Source LLC
Chambersburg PA
CBHW022205020726
47496CB00008B/2895
9783337226251